TOO MANY BUNNIES

by Julie Houston   illustrated by Bob Doty

For Karen, Steven, David, and Brian

PAGES
Publishing Group ™

Second printing by Willowisp Press 1998.

Published by PAGES Publishing Group
801 94th Avenue North, St. Petersburg, Florida 33702

Willowisp Press®

Printed in the United States of America   2 4 6 8 10 9 7 5 3   ISBN 0-87406-906-8

The Bunny family lived underground in a cozy, but very crowded, bunny home.

Benny was the youngest bunny. He was unhappy. His older brothers and sisters never played with him. They said he was too little.

Something else made Benny unhappy, too.

Benny had to do all his chores by himself.

"It's your turn to sweep the floor," said his older sister Betsy.

"It's your turn to wash the dishes," said his bossy sister Betty.

"We're going to play ball," said his brother Bobby. "And you can't play. You're too little."

Benny watched the other bunnies go outside. He was very sad.

"They don't need me," Benny said to himself. "This family has too many bunnies. Maybe I should live some other place and have different brothers and sisters. I'll bet they would play with me."

Benny watched his brothers and sisters play. He had an idea about what to do next.

The next morning Benny got up before all the other bunnies. He packed some crunchy carrots and some green, leafy lettuce in his backpack. Then he tiptoed to the door and was off.

Benny was going to find a new home.

Benny hopped and hopped.

He hopped over to the pond where the turtles were relaxing in the sun. "This would be a great place to live," he thought. He took a carrot out of his backpack.

"Would you like some of my carrot?" Benny asked Tommy Turtle.

"No, thanks," said Tommy. "I just want to lie here in the warm sunshine. Want to join me?"

"You bet!" exclaimed Benny. "Move over!"

The sunshine felt warm as Benny lay on the rock. He liked having a friend.

But after a while, Benny became bored. "It's sunny and nice here," he thought, "but it isn't any fun. I want to play."

Benny decided to leave the turtles and the pond. He strolled to a stream where the beavers were building a dam. "This looks like a nice place to live," he thought.

"May I play with you?" he asked Billy Beaver.

"No time to play now! There's too much work to do! Please, help carry those branches!" shouted Billy.

Benny was excited about helping his new friend.

Benny hopped around until he found a small branch. He carried the branch over to the beaver dam.

"You're in my way!" shouted Billy. Benny almost fell down as Billy flipped and flapped his broad tail in the mud.

"This is not fun for a little bunny," thought Benny. "I could get hurt."

Benny went into the forest to rest.

The next day, Benny hopped into a barnyard. Penny Pig and her brothers were rolling in a big mud puddle. Splat! Squish! Squash! Splash!

"Jump in!" yelled Penny.

"This looks like fun!" Benny said happily. He jumped into the mud and rolled around with his friends.

Benny played in the squishy mud for a while. "What a mess," he thought. "This is no place for a clean little bunny."

It was late and Benny was worried. He came to a fence and sat down. He ate his last carrot.

"Where else can I go to find a new home?" he wondered.

The turtles at the pond were too lazy. The beavers at the dam were too busy. The pigs in the mud were too messy.

All of a sudden, Benny had an idea. "I know the perfect place to live!" he said excitedly.

"I'm home!" called Benny, running into his cozy underground home.

"Oh, Benny, we're so glad to see you!" said Daddy Bunny. He gave Benny a great big bunny hug.

"Benny," said Mother Bunny. "We have a surprise for you. Come in here."

Benny peeked in the room to see . . .

a cute . . . new . . . LITTLE baby brother!

"Now I'm not the littlest bunny!" said Benny.
"I have a little brother to play with. We can
help each other. I like being home!"